The
Witch
at the
Window

BY RUTH CHEW

Illustrations by the author

SCHOLASTIC INC.
New York Toronto London Auckland Sydney Tokyo

ISBN 0-590-41219-1

Reading level is determined by using the Spache Readability Formula. 2.2 signifies high 2nd grade level.

12 11 10 9 8 7 6 5 4 3 2 1   7 8 9/8 0 1/9

Printed in U.S.A.   28

For my niece,
Pauline Patty Chew

1

"Hey, Marge, look at this!" Nick bent down to pick up something that had fallen out of a fat old beech tree.

Marjorie saw that her brother was holding a long-handled wooden spoon. She stared up into the branches overhead. "Hello!" she called. "Is anybody up there?"

There was no answer.

Nick handed Marjorie the spoon. "Maybe somebody left it in the tree."

Marjorie felt the smooth wood. "The wind must have blown it down."

"It's such a big spoon," Nick said, "We could dig with it at the beach."

"Mother doesn't like us to take things that don't belong to us," Marjorie reminded him.

"But if we leave the spoon here in the park," Nick said, "somebody else will pick it up. Then the person who owns it will never get it back."

Marjorie thought for a minute. "We can keep it safe in case we find out who lost it." She tucked the big spoon under her arm.

"I'm getting hungry," Nick said.

Marjorie looked at the blue sky. "I wonder what time it is."

"We'd better not be late for supper again." Nick began to walk along the narrow path that went through the woods on Lookout Mountain.

The two children had spent the afternoon in Prospect Park. Now they went around the big hill until they came to the road that went through the park. Marjorie took a look at the traffic. "It must be rush hour."

While they waited for the light to turn green, Nick and Marjorie heard a clear, high whistle.

Nick looked around. "What was that, Marge?"

"It's that bird, there. Come on. The light's changing." Marjorie walked quickly across the road.

Nick ran after her. "Marge," he said, "the bird followed us." He pointed to the lowest branch of a chestnut tree.

Marjorie laughed. "What makes you think it's the same bird, Nick?"

"It looks exactly like the one that was whistling at us on the other side of the road," Nick said.

"That's a starling," Marjorie told him.

"There are lots of them in Brooklyn. And they all look alike."

The bird was about as big as a robin. It was fat and had a short tail. In the sunlight its black feathers gleamed with purple and green lights.

"It's beautiful!" Nick said.

Marjorie nodded. "I never really looked hard at a starling before." She took a step toward the bird.

The starling flapped up into the branches of the chestnut tree.

"You scared it, Marge," Nick said.

"I only wanted to get a better look," Marjorie told him.

"Well, if all starlings look alike, you'll have another chance." Nick started running toward the park gate.

Marjorie raced after him.

2

Marjorie and Nick lived four long blocks from the park. They ran along Ocean Parkway and turned the corner onto Church Avenue. By the time they reached East Fifth Street both of them were out of breath.

They stopped running and walked halfway down the block.

Nick looked up into the big sycamore tree in front of their house. He grabbed his sister's arm. "Marge, there's that spooky bird! It *is* following us."

"Don't be silly, Nick. I told you

there are lots of starlings in Brooklyn."
Marjorie climbed the front stoop of
the old stone house. Nick came up
after her. Marjorie's house key was
on a string around her neck. She
unlocked the front door.

Their father came into the hall. He
hugged both Marjorie and Nick at the
same time. "You just made it, kids,"
Mr. Gordon said. "Any minute now
I would have had to set the table.
Isn't that your job, Nick?"

Marjorie ran upstairs and hid the
big wooden spoon in the bottom drawer
of her dresser. Then she washed her
hands and went down to the kitchen
to help her mother.

At suppertime Marjorie said, "We
saw a starling in the park. I never
knew they were such pretty birds."

Mrs. Gordon put a carrot stick on

Nick's plate. "In some countries starlings are kept in cages."

"That's awful," Marjorie said. "Birds should be flying around. Why would anybody put one in a cage?"

"Maybe because starlings can be taught to talk," her mother said.

"Like parrots?" Nick asked.

"Don't get any ideas, Nick," Mrs. Gordon said. "I don't like birds in cages any more than Marjorie does."

"Maybe we wouldn't have to keep it in a cage," Nick said. "It could just fly from room to room."

Mrs. Gordon put down her fork. "I'm sorry, Nick. I don't want you bringing any birds into the house. They belong outdoors."

After supper, everybody went into the living room. "*King Kong* is on television tonight," Nick said.

His mother laughed. "You don't want to see that old movie."

"Yes, we do," Nick said.

"It will give you nightmares," Mrs. Gordon said.

"Dad can watch it with us." Nick turned on the television. "He can turn it off if we get scared."

Mrs. Gordon picked up her library book. "I'm warning you. If either of you children wakes up screaming tonight, you'll both go without television for the rest of the week."

Marjorie had never liked scary movies, but she didn't want Nick to know it. He was younger than she was. She sat down on the sofa beside her father.

The movie wasn't nearly as scary as Marjorie had thought it would be. Maybe that was because her friends had told her how it ended.

When the movie was over, Mrs. Gordon closed her book. "Bedtime, Nick."

Nick went upstairs to take a shower and brush his teeth. Then it was Marjorie's turn.

3

"Marge, wake up!"

Marjorie opened her eyes. In the darkness she saw Nick standing beside her bed. "What's the matter?"

"Somebody's outside my window, trying to get in," Nick said.

Marjorie sat up in bed. "Sh-sh! Don't let Mother hear you."

King Kong must have been too scary for Nick after all, Marjorie thought. And if Mrs. Gordon knew Nick had a nightmare, Marjorie wouldn't be allowed to watch her favorite program on Saturday. "I'll go to your room and see what's going on," she told her brother.

Marjorie slipped out of bed and started down the hall. Nick tiptoed after her. His room was at the very end of the hall. As Marjorie came closer to it, she heard a creaky noise.

She reached the doorway. The noise was coming from the window. Marjorie's heart started to pound. A little cold shiver crawled up her back.

She took a deep breath. Then she walked over to the window. Nick came right behind.

Marjorie wasn't tall enough to see over the air conditioner that was in the window. She looked around the shadowy room. "Where's your chair?" she whispered.

Nick went to get his desk chair. Marjorie stepped onto it and lifted one slat of the venetian blind.

Nick climbed up beside her. The two children peeked through the crack in the blind.

They saw two feet in shoes with big buckles on them. The feet were standing on the air conditioner outside. Two thin, bony hands were trying to push up the window Mr. Gordon had taped shut.

Marjorie grabbed the venetian blind cord. She pulled the blind all the way up to the top of the tall window. Now Nick and Marjorie could see that there was a woman on the air conditioner. She was wearing a long dress and a pointed hat with a wide brim.

"Marge, it's a witch!" Nick gasped.

The woman was so surprised when the blind was pulled up that she nearly lost her balance. She grabbed hold of the window to steady herself. Then she pressed her long nose against the

glass and tried to look into the room.

Marjorie and Nick jumped off the chair and ran. At the door of the room Marjorie turned to look back at the window.

"Nick, she's gone!" Marjorie said.

The sky outside was slowly turning gray. And there was no sign of the witch at the window.

4

"Hey, Marge, it's getting to be morning!" Nick walked back to the window. He climbed on the chair so he could see over the air conditioner. There was a faint pink glow over the roofs of the stores on Church Avenue now.

Marjorie came over and got up on the chair beside her brother. She looked down into the little backyard. A starling was splashing in the birdbath.

The sun began to rise over the apartment buildings in the distance.

"I wonder where the witch went," Marjorie said.

"Do you think we ought to tell Mom and Dad about her?" Nick asked.

Marjorie shook her head. "They'd think we were making it up. You know Daddy says witches aren't real."

"Mom might think the witch was a nightmare," Nick said. "I guess we'd better not say anything about her."

Marjorie and Nick stood at the window and watched the sunrise. They looked in all the backyards to see if the witch might be hiding in one of them. But they didn't see her.

The sky was blue now. A little breeze made the yellow roses on the fence bob up and down.

"Let's go in the yard." Nick stepped down from the chair. He went to get a pair of jeans out of his dresser.

"Sh-sh! Mother and Daddy are still asleep." Marjorie tiptoed to her room to get dressed.

They slid down the bannister and walked through the house to the kitchen. Nick opened the back door. "Hey, look what's in the magnolia tree!"

A black starling with a yellow beak sat on one of the lowest branches. It was shaking its wings. Drops of water splashed all around.

"Wouldn't it be fun to teach a bird like that to talk?" Nick went out into the yard. Marjorie slipped out after him.

Nick walked quietly over to the magnolia tree. He stepped onto the bottom bar of the fence. From there he climbed to the top bar. Now he could reach a branch of the tree. Nick pulled himself up onto it.

The starling was still shaking water from its wings. Nick was splashed in the face. He reached up for the bird.

"Keep your dirty hands off me!" The starling hopped out of his reach.

Nick was so surprised he nearly fell out of the tree.

Marjorie came running down the flagstone path. "Leave the bird alone, Nick. And come down from there. You know Mother told us not to climb the tree."

Nick was holding tight to the branch. "Marge, did you hear that? I don't have to teach this bird to talk. It talks as well as I do."

"Better," the starling told him.

Marjorie looked up at the black bird. Its feathers shone in the sunlight. "It's so beautiful!" she said. "Someone must have kept it for a pet."

The starling tipped its head to one side and looked at Marjorie. "For a minute I thought you had some sense. But now I see you're just as stupid as your brother."

5

Nick glared at the starling. "Why do you have to be so nasty?"

"Your mother doesn't want you in this tree," the bird snapped. "And neither do I. Get out of it this minute."

There was a shrill whistling sound. The starling looked around to see where it was coming from. The noise stopped suddenly.

The bird hopped higher in the magnolia tree. "What was that?"

"Mother's teakettle," Marjorie said. "She must be in the kitchen."

Nick crawled along the branch to the trunk of the tree. He slid down the trunk to the ground.

Marjorie looked up into the magnolia. The starling was high in the tree now, and the leaves were so thick that the bird was hidden from sight.

Nick sniffed the air. "I smell bacon." He walked toward the house. "Come on, Marge." He opened the back door.

Mrs. Gordon was bending over a frying pan. "I thought you two were still asleep. What in the world were you doing in the yard at this hour?"

"There was a starling out there," Nick told her.

Mrs. Gordon laughed. "Only one?"

"Don't laugh, Mom," Nick said. "I wanted to catch it and teach it to talk, but it already knew how."

"Are you sure?" his mother asked.

"Nick's telling the truth," Marjorie said. "A bird *was* talking to us."

Mr. Gordon walked into the kitchen. Mrs. Gordon began to take the bacon out of the frying pan and put it on a plate. "Listen to this, John," she said. "The children were talking to a starling in the yard this morning."

"That's not a bad way to start the day," Mr. Gordon said. "It's almost as good as bacon for breakfast."

"How do you want your eggs?" Mrs. Gordon asked.

After breakfast Mr. and Mrs. Gordon both left for work.

Marjorie made her bed and walked down the hall to Nick's room. He was sitting on the floor with a big red book in his lap.

"What are you looking up?" Marjorie asked.

"Starlings," Nick told her. "I found out they build their nests in hollow trees. This book doesn't say anything about them being able to talk."

"Let's go to the park," Marjorie said.

"Great idea." Nick put the book on his desk. "I want to climb that big tree the spoon fell out of."

6

Nick and Marjorie walked along the shady, tree-lined streets to Prospect Park. It was cool and quiet there. No cars were allowed in the park during the summer, except at rush hours.

Four ducks were swimming near the shore of the lake. Nick ran over to get a better look at them. The ducks swam away toward the little island.

A young man jogged down the road-way. Two old ladies sat on a bench and talked. Marjorie stopped to watch a pair of squirrels playing tag.

"Hurry up, Marge." Nick began to walk around the lake. Marjorie ran to catch up with him. They started up the path that went around Lookout Mountain.

"What are these things on the ground?" Nick bent down and picked up a purple berry.

"That looks like a blackberry," Marjorie said, "but there aren't any blackberry bushes here." She caught sight of a small tree that overhung the path. "That's where they're coming from."

Nick stared at the tree. It was covered with berries. A bird sat on one of the branches. "Here's another starling, Marge. You're right. They do all look alike."

The bird stretched its wings and glared at Nick. It opened its beak and said, "How can you be so stupid? I'm not in the least like any other bird."

Marjorie took a step toward the little tree. "Then you must be the same starling that was in our yard this morning."

"What if I am?" The bird fluttered to a higher branch and pecked at a berry.

"Are those things good to eat?" Nick asked.

"Of course, stupid," the starling said. "Don't you know a mulberry tree when you see one?"

Marjorie decided not to waste her time talking to such a rude bird. "Come on, Nick. I thought you wanted to climb that tree."

Nick followed Marjorie along the path.

The starling came flapping after them. "Didn't you say your mother doesn't want you to climb trees?"

Marjorie didn't answer.

"Mom doesn't want us to climb the *magnolia*," Nick told the bird. "She thinks we'll break it. We're going to climb a much bigger tree."

The starling flew down onto the

ground in front of the children. "Why don't you go to the zoo and watch the sea lions? That's much more fun than climbing trees. Those animals do tricks at feeding time."

"We saw the sea lions last week." Marjorie stepped off the path to walk around the bird. Nick came after her.

The starling fluttered up into the air again. It flew just over the children's heads. Now and then the bird sat on a tree branch beside the path. All the time it kept watching Nick and Marjorie with bright dark eyes.

They made their way through a tangled patch of honeysuckle and around a bend in the path.

"Here it is!" Nick pointed to a large beech tree growing on the side of the hill.

7

The trunk of the tree was covered with names and dates. Someone had cut KS L MT into the smooth gray bark and carved a heart around it.

"June 1902," Marjorie read. "The tree must have been here for ages."

"Longer than that." The starling flew over to perch on the lowest branch.

"Take a look at this, Marge." Nick pointed to some words cut deep into the tree.

STELLA'S TREE
KEEP OFF

Marjorie felt the thick ridge of bark around the S. "I wonder who Stella was."

"What do you mean by *was*?" the starling squawked.

Marjorie looked up at the bird. Maybe it wasn't the starling's fault that it was so rude, she thought. Whoever taught it to talk had forgotten to teach it manners.

"This carving looks much older than what was done in 1902," Marjorie said.

"The person who put it here must have died long ago."

The starling opened its yellow beak, but for a moment it didn't speak. Then it said, "That's the silliest thing I ever heard!"

Marjorie reached high over her head. She grabbed hold of the branch and pulled herself up onto it.

The starling flew down to the ground. "Why do you want to climb *that* tree? Those rotten old branches will break under you. The best tree to climb is an oak. I'll show you one that's right on top of Lookout Mountain. You can see all of Brooklyn from there."

Marjorie hooked her legs around the branch. "Come on up here, Nick." She reached down to grab her brother's hand.

Marjorie helped Nick until he reached the branch. After that he could climb on his own. The branches were fairly close together.

A breeze rustled the shiny little leaves of the beech tree. The sunlight was broken into little patches that seemed to dance all around the children.

"It's lovely up here," Marjorie said. "Why didn't the starling want us to climb this tree?"

Nick put his arms around the trunk and swung himself to the other side of it. "I think I've found the reason, Marge. Look at this."

Marjorie worked her way around the tree.

Nick pulled aside a clump of leaves to show her a large hole in the trunk. "My guess is that the starling has a nest in the tree. Maybe there are baby birds in it."

"Leave it alone, Nick," Marjorie said.

"I just want to peek at it." Nick looked into the hole. "It's pretty deep. I don't see a nest."

Nick sat on the edge of the hole and let his legs hang down inside it. "This makes a great seat! You ought to try it, Marge."

Suddenly the bark crumbled under Nick. Before Marjorie knew what was happening, he slid out of sight into the hole in the tree.

8

"Didn't I tell you to stay out of this tree?" a harsh voice said.

Marjorie saw that the starling was perched on a nearby twig. She didn't answer the bird. Instead she looked down into the dark hole.

"Nick," she called, "are you all right?"

"I'm not hurt, if that's what you mean," he said. "My feet are jammed against one side of the tree trunk and my back against the other. I guess I'll be all right for a little while."

"I'll go home and get a rope." Marjorie started climbing down the tree. It was much harder than climbing up. She was afraid she'd get dizzy if she looked down. It seemed a long time before she came to the lowest branch. Marjorie dropped to the ground and rolled over and over.

She jumped to her feet and began to race down the path around Lookout Mountain. She ran past the mulberry tree, along the lakeshore, across the roadway, and over to the big iron park gate. Here Marjorie slowed to a walk and crossed the wide street outside the park. She decided to jog the rest of the way home.

Marjorie ran up the steps of her house and opened the door with her key. She remembered that her mother had a clothesline somewhere in the basement. Mrs. Gordon used it when the dryer was out of order.

Marjorie found the rope behind the laundry room door. Her mother always wound the clothesline around a stick to keep it from getting tangled. The stick had snapped in half and fallen out onto the floor.

Marjorie tore upstairs to her room. She took her little square flashlight off her night table and dropped it into the pocket of her jeans. Then she took the big wooden spoon out of her dresser drawer. She carried it down to the laundry room and wound the clothesline around it.

Marjorie held tight to the big spoon and jogged back to the park. The young man was still jogging along the roadway. He waved to Marjorie. "Isn't this great? This is my third time around."

Marjorie waved back. She crossed the road and jogged along the lake-shore. A duck with four ducklings went paddling by. Marjorie would have liked to stop and look at them, but she kept jogging until she came to the path up the big hill. Then she began to run.

When she came to the beech tree, Marjorie tossed the rope over the lowest branch and used it to pull herself up. She wound the rope back onto the spoon and started up the tree.

The starling was still sitting on the same twig. "Here comes your sister now, Nick," it called down into the hole in the tree. "You should be out of there in no time."

The bird stared at the spoon under Marjorie's arm. But it didn't say anything.

Marjorie tied one end of the clothesline to a branch with the square knot her father had taught her. The rest of the rope was still wound around the wooden spoon.

Marjorie thought for a minute. If she let the rope down into the tree it might get caught on something and never reach Nick.

She turned on her flashlight. Marjorie held the flashlight in one hand and the spoon in the other. As she slowly let herself down into the hollow tree, the rope unwound from the spoon.

9

"Why don't you just pull your brother out?" the starling screamed. "This way you'll both get stuck down there!"

Majorie held tight to the spoon and inched her way down into the hollow tree. The little flashlight glowed in the darkness.

Nick looked up at his sister. "I came down a lot faster than that, Marge."

"I feel like a caterpillar," Marjorie told him.

When she reached Nick, he grabbed hold of the rope too.

"You climb up first," Marjorie said. "You've been down here long enough."

"I kind of got used to it, Marge," Nick looked at the wooden spoon. There was still a lot of rope wound around it. "Let's go all the way down this hole. I'd like to see what's at the bottom."

Marjorie shone the flashlight into the hole. "It looks like a lot of tree roots." She started working her way down.

Nick was close beside her. The inside of the tree was twisted and lumpy.

They moved from one lump to the next. It was like going down a rough stairway.

Something fluttered past Marjorie's ear. She jumped back, still holding onto the clothesline. "Nick, that wasn't a baby starling!"

"Maybe it was a bat," Nick said.

Marjorie began to wish she were back outside in the sunshine. But she didn't want Nick to think she was afraid. Anyway, they were getting close to the bottom of the hole.

A few feet farther down, Marjorie's feet touched the ground. At the same time the last of the clothesline unwound. She began to shine the flashlight all around. "This is like a little cave."

Nick let go of the rope and left it dangling. "Marge," he whispered, "look!"

Marjorie saw a narrow door set among the thick roots of the tree. It was open just wide enough for her to see a faint red glow on the other side of it.

Both children stood quite still. They listened for any sound, but all they heard was their own breathing.

Nick took a step toward the door. He peeked through the opening. Then he gave the door a push. It didn't move.

Marjorie leaned her shoulder against the door and shoved hard. The door creaked open.

"There's nobody here," Nick said. "Let's explore this place, Marge."

The two children stepped through the doorway into the cave on the other side.

10

Marjorie looked around. The yellow light of her flashlight showed a big iron pot set over a bed of glowing embers. Pale gray steam rose out of the pot, but no smoke came from the red coals.

She flashed the light over the uneven dirt walls. "I don't see any door to the outside, but somebody must live here." Marjorie pointed to a tattered blanket thrown over a pile of dry leaves. "There's the bed."

A big table stood in the middle of the cave. Nick sat down on a three-legged stool next to it. He opened a large book on the table. "Look at this, Marge."

Marjorie went to shine her flashlight on it. She saw a bookplate inside the front cover. "This book belongs to Stella," Marjorie read.

"*Stella* was the name cut into the tree," Nick reminded her.

Marjorie began to turn the pages of the book. They were dog-eared and stained. Some of them were stuck together. "It looks like a cookbook."

She started to read. "Nick! These aren't recipes. They're magic spells!"

Nick leaned over the book. "Now's our chance! Maybe we can work one." He started turning the pages.

Majorie looked over his shoulder. The flashlight seemed to be getting dim. She could barely make out the words.

"It's no use," Nick said. "To make yourself invisible, you have to have six tigers' teeth and a cup of sand from the Sahara desert."

"You're right." Marjorie shut the book. "We could never do those spells. Anyway, we need steaming brew to make them work."

"Maybe that's brew in the big pot," Nick said.

The light from the flashlight was very faint now. In a few seconds it was just a spark. Then it went out.

"I must have had it turned on too long." Marjorie put the little square flashlight on the table.

The cave was very dark now. There was only the red glow from under the pot.

Marjorie was quiet. She was thinking. When she spoke it was in a whisper. "Nick," she said. "I read in that book that you have to use a special spoon to work those spells. It's a *wooden* spoon. The book says it's something every *witch* must own."

Nick tried to see into the dark corners of the cave. "Stella must be a witch!"

"And we've got her spoon," Marjorie said. "That's why she was trying to get into our house. She can't work her magic without it."

Nick reached for the spoon. "Let me have that for a minute, Marge."

"Be careful what you do with it." Marjorie handed the spoon to her brother.

Nick picked up the flashlight and walked over to the iron pot. He put the flashlight on the bowl of the big wooden spoon. Then he lowered it into the dark, steaming brew. It started to hiss and sizzle.

"One," Nick counted, "two, three —" When he came to "seven," a light began to glow down in the depths. Nick raised the spoon out of the pot. He grabbed the flashlight and waved it in the air.

It was brighter than Marjorie had ever seen it before.

"How's that for magic?" Nick grinned. "I think I'll write this spell in Stella's book."

11

"Give that to me, Nick. We'd better take care of it." Marjorie took the spoon.

Nick set the flashlight on the table. It was so bright now that it lit up the whole cave. He walked over to a shelf that was cut into one of the dirt walls.

"Hey, Marge—look at all these bottles and boxes!"

"Maybe that's where Stella keeps her food," Marjorie said.

Nick picked up a dusty green bottle and shook it. The bottle rattled. He unscrewed the cap and poured something into his hand. "Stella must have broken a plate."

Marjorie came over. "That's not broken china, Nick. Those are teeth."

Nick took a good look. "Great big cats' teeth," he said. "Tigers' teeth?" He put them back into the bottle and screwed on the cap.

Marjorie started to look at the other things on the shelf. "There aren't any labels." She peeked into a little cardboard box. "Ick! Mouse tails."

"Here's a bag with a label, *Domino Sugar*." Nick opened the yellow paper bag and put a few grains on the end of his tongue. He spat them out at once.

"It's not sugar, or salt. Hey, Marge! Maybe it's Sahara sand!" Nick put down the bag and ran over to the table in the middle of the cave. He began to look through the big book.

"I suppose you're looking for the spell that makes you invisible," Marjorie said.

"Yes," Nick told her. "I know I saw it in this book."

"Maybe it's listed under *disappearing*," Marjorie said.

"That would be near the beginning of the book," Nick said. "I know it wasn't there."

"Look under *vanishing*," Marjorie suggested. Secretly she was just as eager as Nick to learn this magic trick.

Nick turned to the last pages of the book. "Here we are!" He read the spell. "We ought to be able to do it, Marge. You have to put the teeth and the sand and your favorite finger ring into a bag. Then you tie the bag to the spoon with a brand-new shoelace. Your stir them around in the brew while you count to twenty-one."

Marjorie thought for a minute. "I don't have a favorite finger ring. Do you?"

"No." Nick looked at the book again. "There's one of those little starry things next to *ring*."

Marjorie came over to look at the book. She saw another little star at

the bottom of the page. Beside it in tiny letters was printed *or another small metal object worn every day.* "Read this, Nick. Maybe we can do the spell with my house key."

"How about the brand-new shoelace?" Nick said. "Mine are worn out, and yours don't look much better. How much do shoelaces cost?"

"Didn't you just invent a magic spell that mends things?" Marjorie sat down on the dirt floor and took the lace out of one of her sneakers.

She tied the shoelace to the witch's spoon and dipped it into the big iron pot. The brew began to sizzle. Marjorie counted to seven. When she brought up the spoon, the shoelace was bright and new with a shiny tip on each end.

12

"Maybe Stella has a measuring cup."
Marjorie went to look among the boxes
and jars on the shelf. She found a
teacup with a broken handle. Marjorie
filled it to the brim with sand from
the yellow paper bag.

Nick watched her. "How are we
going to get a bag for the spell? That
Domino Sugar sack would fall apart
in the brew."

Marjorie was carrying the teacup
over to the table. On the way the
sneaker without a shoelace fell off.
Marjorie set the cup on the table and
went to get her shoe.

She was about to shove her foot
into the sneaker when she caught sight

of her sock. Marjorie pulled it off and shoved her bare foot into the sneaker. "Go get six tigers' teeth, Nick."

The sock was a stretchy one. Marjorie poured the sand into it. Nick dropped in the teeth, one at a time. Then Marjorie took the key from around her neck and pushed it into the sock. She left the string on it and pushed that in too.

The sock was bulging. Nick held it while Marjorie tied it to the wooden spoon with the bright new shoelace. She twisted the lace several times around the spoon and the sock. And then she made a double bow.

"Now for the spell!" Nick said.

Marjorie carried the spoon with the heavy sock tied to it over to the iron pot. Slowly she let it down into the steaming witch's brew.

The steam turned yellow and then

green. The brew foamed up. Marjorie
was afraid it would boil over.

"Don't forget to stir," Nick reminded her.

Marjorie counted to twenty-one, giving a wide stir with each number.

"Stop!" Nick said.

Marjorie hauled up the spoon with
the dripping sock. She walked over
and laid it on the table in the middle
of the cave.

Nick came after her. "Marge, look at the shoelace."

Marjorie stared at it. The lace was stained and the tips were frayed.

"It's just the way it was before we enchanted it," Marjorie said. She began to untie the double bow. It took her quite a while because the shoelace was soaking wet, but at last she managed to undo it.

Marjorie dumped everything out of her sock onto the table. "Nick," she said, "the desert sand is still dry and so are the tigers' teeth!"

"Where's your key?" Nick asked.

"I don't know." Marjorie looked at the sand scattered across the table. She counted all the tigers' teeth, but she didn't see the key. "Mother will have a fit when she finds out I've lost it."

"What'll we do, Marge?" Nick asked.

"We can't get into our house without the key. I'm hungry. It must be lunch time."

Marjorie sat down on the dirt floor and put on the wet sock. She laced the old shoelace back into her shoe. "We'll have to do without lunch. Let's go home and wait for Mother and Dad." She stood up and took a look at the table. "Before we go, we'd better put everything away."

Nick went to get the Domino Sugar sack. Marjorie picked up the tigers' teeth. She dusted the sand off each one and dropped them all into the green bottle. With her hand she brushed the sand into a neat pile at the edge of the table.

Marjorie felt something hard in the sand. She took hold of it. "Nick, here's the key!"

13

Marjorie held up the key by the string and swung it in front of her brother. "I don't know why I couldn't find it before."

Nick had a strange look on his face. He seemed to be looking right through Marjorie. Suddenly he started to laugh.

"What's wrong with you, Nick?" Marjorie asked.

"Marge, the spell worked!" Nick said. "But not the way we wanted it to. The key vanished. And so have you!"

Marjorie looked at the key swinging from her hand. "I don't know what you're talking about."

"Don't argue, Marge." Nick held out his hand. "Just give me the key for a minute."

Marjorie dropped the key into Nick's hand. When she let go of the string, she couldn't see it anymore. And she couldn't see Nick, either. She blinked. Then she understood. "Now do you see the key, Nick?"

"Yes," Nick said. "And I can see you too."

"But now I can't see you, or the key," Marjorie told him.

"You can have the key back, Marge." Nick put it in her hand. At once she could see him.

Marjorie hung the key around her neck. She picked up the Domino Sugar bag with one hand and held it just below the edge of the table. With her other hand Marjorie swept the desert sand into the bag. "Can you see what I'm doing, Nick?"

"I see the sand moving itself into the sugar bag," Nick said. "It looks weird."

"Then it's just the key, not everything I touch, that disappears." Marjorie took the bag of sand and the
bottle of tigers' teeth back to the shelf
where they had found them.

"Your clothes are invisible," Nick
said. "What happens if you put something into your pocket?"

The wooden spoon was on the table.
Marjorie went over and picked it up.
Nick watched the spoon rise from the
table.

"This is too big to go in my pocket," Marjorie said.

"It's gone, Marge. What did you do with it?" Nick asked.

"I tucked it under my shirt." Marjorie started to turn the pages of the big book.

"Cut it out, Marge. You're giving me the creeps," Nick said. "It looks as if those pages are flipping over all by themselves."

Marjorie took the key from around her neck and laid it on the table. "Is that better?"

"Much," Nick said. "I can see you now. What are you looking for in the book?"

"There's something I always wanted to do," Marjorie said, "ever since I saw *Peter Pan* on television."

14

Nick grabbed the book and started looking through it.

Marjorie laughed. "I thought you were hungry."

"I am," Nick said. "But we'd get home for lunch much quicker if we could fly. Hey! Here's the spell to do it."

Marjorie leaned over his shoulder. "It looks easy. All we need are seven feathers, each one a different color."

"I once found a blue jay's feather in the yard," Nick said. "But I don't have it anymore."

"I'll see if Stella has any feathers." Marjorie went over to the shelf in the wall. She took the lid off a box.

"Spiderwebs." She peeked in all the other boxes and jars. "There's nothing that even looks like a feather here," Marjorie said. "Let's go home."

Marjorie went back to the table to get her flashlight. "Where's the key, Nick? I left it right here."

Nick shut the book of spells. He began to run his hand over the top of the table. Marjorie watched him. "Oh, I forgot. The key is invisible until you touch it."

All at once Nick disappeared.

"I see you found it," Marjorie said. "Would you mind wearing it on the way home? I have to hold the flashlight, and it bothers you to see things like that moving around."

"Let me be first up the rope," Nick said.

"All right. Just tell me when you're out of here," Marjorie said.

"Here I go!" Marjorie heard Nick's voice from outside the door. She looked around Stella's cave to make sure everything was in the right place. She went out and closed the door behind her.

The flashlight lit up the tangled roots in the dark hole under the tree. Marjorie saw the clothesline dangling down. It was jumping as if it were alive.

"It's harder going up than it was coming down," she heard Nick say. "There's not much light coming down. Shine the flashlight over here, Marge."

Marjorie turned the flashlight toward where she thought Nick was. "How's that?"

"A little higher," he said.

Marjorie pointed the flashlight about four feet above her head.

"That's fine," Nick told her.

Marjorie began to shinny up the rope. It wasn't easy to do with the flashlight in her hand. When she came to the first twisted lump inside the tree, she decided to stop and rest.

"Ow! Get off my foot, Marge." Nick was already on the lump.

"If you want to go up the rope first, Nick," Marjorie said, "you'd better give me the key, so I can see where you are."

"Okay," Nick said. "Hold still and I'll hang it around your neck."

Marjorie clung to the rope. She felt the string slip over her head. Now she could see her brother.

Nick began climbing the rope again.

Marjorie came after him with the flashlight.

15

When Nick reached the top of the hole, he climbed out onto a branch of the beech tree. The starling was perched on a nearby twig.

"Hello," Nick said. "Are you still here?"

"That's a stupid question," the bird said. "Do I look as if I'm somewhere else? Anyway, I have as much right to be here as you do. Maybe more."

Marjorie turned off her flashlight and put it into her pocket. Then she crawled out of the hole in the tree. She sat down on the branch beside Nick.

"Where's your sister?" the starling asked. The bird was looking right at Marjorie.

Marjorie thought it would be fun

to play a trick on it. She took the key off her neck and slipped the string over Nick's head.

"Awk!" The starling stared first at Marjorie and then at the place where Nick had been a moment before.

It looked so surprised that Marjorie couldn't help laughing.

"Oh, there you are, Marge," Nick said. "I thought it was about time you got out of the tree." Suddenly he stopped talking and just stared at her. "I can *see* you! Did you drop the key?"

"No. I just gave it back to you." Marjorie untied the clothesline from the branch and took the big wooden spoon out from under her shirt. Then she began to wind the rope around the spoon.

The starling watched everything.

Marjorie finished winding up the

clothesline. She tucked the wooden spoon under her arm. "Come on, Nick. Let's go."

There was no answer.

Marjorie reached out to touch her brother's arm. She felt only air. "Nick," she yelled, "where are you?"

"I'm down here on the ground already," Nick shouted. "What's taking you so long?"

Marjorie started down the tree. It was easier than when she climbed down to go home for the rope. Marjorie didn't step on any weak branches. And this time she didn't hurry. When she got to the bottom she slid down the trunk of the tree.

Marjorie landed on her feet and started walking quickly along the path. She heard footsteps behind her.

"Aren't you going to wait for me?" Nick asked.

"You didn't wait for me," Marjorie told him. "And you scared me. You'd better not do anything like that again with the magic key."

"Don't be mad, Marge. You were playing tricks yourself," Nick reminded her. "I know what's wrong with you," he said. "You're hungry. You'll feel much better after lunch."

"So would I—if I had any lunch," a voice croaked.

Marjorie and Nick looked up. The starling was sitting on the branch of a young oak tree. "I'm sick of mulberries," the bird said. "What are you going to eat?"

"Whatever Mom left for us in the refrigerator," Nick said.

Marjorie was sorry now that she'd played a trick on the bird. "Would you like to join us for lunch?" she said.

"Don't mind if I do." The starling flew down and perched on the end of the wooden spoon.

Marjorie and Nick took the bird home with them.

16

Nick unlocked the front door of the house.

Marjorie went inside with the starling on the spoon. "Give me the key, Nick."

A moment later she felt the key in her hand, and she could see her brother. Marjorie hung the key around her neck.

"Now that you are invisible," Nick told her, "the bird seems to be riding on a flying spoon."

"Oh!" the starling said. "I wish I could see that."

Marjorie walked over to the big round mirror in the hall.

The bird stretched its wings, cocked its head, and stared into the mirror. "I'm not such a bad-looking bird after all."

"Don't you know what you look like?" Nick asked.

"I've tried to see myself in the lake," the starling told him. "But it's full of beer cans and waterweed."

Marjorie looked into the mirror. She couldn't see herself at all, but the black starling and the wooden spoon

seemed to be floating in mid-air. The bird looked like a witch on a broom.

Marjorie remembered that her mother didn't want birds in the house. "Nick, how about taking our guest into the yard? We could have a picnic on the table there."

Nick tried to lift the starling off the spoon.

"Don't bother," the starling said. "I don't mind staying on the spoon. Just set me on the picnic table."

"I have to put Mother's clothesline away." Marjorie took the spoon and Nick picked up the starling and went outside.

Marjorie went down to the laundry room. She unwound the clothesline and put it away. Then she ran upstairs and hid the spoon in her dresser drawer. She took the key off her neck and set it on the little glass tray on her dresser. As soon as Marjorie let go of it, the key disappeared.

Down in the kitchen, Marjorie looked in the refrigerator. She found a bowl of red Jell-O and a plate with a hunk of meat loaf on it. Marjorie put them on a big tray with a container of milk, three peaches, a loaf of bread, and a jar of peanut butter. She added paper cups and napkins.

Marjorie opened the kitchen drawer and took out silverware for the picnic. She caught sight of the very small spoon her mother used to eat soft-boiled eggs. Marjorie put it on the tray too.

She went to get a plastic tablecloth from the buffet in the dining room. Then she carried the heavy tray out into the backyard.

17

The picnic table was in a shady place near the back fence. Marjorie spread the cloth on it and set three places. "Lunch is ready!" she called.

Nick was trying to fill the birdbath with the garden hose. The water spurted from the nozzle. It splashed out of the birdbath and all over Nick. "Sorry," he said to the starling on the edge of the birdbath.

The bird was even wetter than Nick. It shook the water from its black feathers. "You did me a favor, Nick. I was much too hot. Now I'm nice and cool."

Nick pulled off his sneakers and left them to dry in the sun. He hung his shirt on a rose bush. Then he walked over to the picnic table and sat down on a bench. "Come on," he yelled to the bird. "You can get a drink now."

The starling flew across the yard. Marjorie poured a little milk into a paper cup and held it for the bird to drink.

The starling was very thirsty. It kept on drinking until the cup was empty. Then it looked at Marjorie. "Nice of you to help me. I haven't tasted milk for a long time."

Nick was spreading peanut butter on a slice of bread. He broke off a little piece and held it out to the starling.

The bird stood on one foot and took the bit of bread with the other. "Thank you, Nick."

Marjorie wondered if she'd heard right. Somebody must have taught the starling manners after all!

The bird pecked at the peanut butter for a few minutes. "This stuff sticks to the roof of my beak."

Marjorie was making a meat loaf sandwich for herself. "Maybe you'd like some of this." She cut off a little slice of meat loaf.

The starling tried to pick up a fork. "Marjorie, would you please hold this for me? It's just a bit too big."

Marjorie held the fork with the meat loaf on it so the starling could take a bite. She ate her sandwich at the same time. "Meat loaf is Daddy's favorite. How do you like it?"

The starling wiped its beak with a

paper napkin. "It's even better than beetles' whiskers."

When it was time for dessert, Marjorie used the big tablespoon to fill three paper cups with Jell-O. She took a teaspoon for herself, gave one to Nick, and handed her mother's tiny egg spoon to the starling.

The bird hopped onto the rim of the paper cup.

"Take it easy!" Nick grabbed the cup just in time to keep it from tipping over. Then he and Marjorie took turns holding it so the starling could eat.

At first the bird had a little trouble with the spoon. But soon it was happily scooping Jell-O out of the cup. "Eating from a spoon keeps my feathers from getting sticky," the starling said.

18

When lunch was over, Marjorie and Nick cleared the picnic table and put everything on the big tray. The starling stacked the dirty paper cups one inside the other.

"What are you going to do this afternoon?" the starling asked.

"I'm tired of climbing up and down that beech tree," Marjorie said. "Maybe we'll go to the zoo after all."

"Well, have fun!" The bird fluttered up into the magnolia tree. "Thanks for the lunch." It stretched its wings and then flew up over the rooftops and out of sight.

Nick's shirt and sneakers were dry now. He put them on. "That bird turned out to be pretty nice once you got to know it."

"Maybe all along it was just hungry." Marjorie handed him the folded tablecloth. "This goes in the dining room drawer." She carried the tray into the house.

"I'll get the key." Marjorie ran upstairs and felt in the little glass tray. As soon as her fingers touched the key, she could see it. Marjorie hung it around her neck and went downstairs.

The clock in the front hall struck two. "We'd better hurry," Marjorie said. "The zoo closes at four."

Nick was sitting on the bottom landing of the stairs. He jumped to his feet. "Don't sneak up on me like that! Where are you anyway?"

"Right here." Marjorie touched his elbow. "Come on." She opened the door.

They headed back to the park. The

zoo was all the way over on the other side by Flatbush Avenue.

The hot sun beat down on their heads.

"Why do you want to go to the zoo all of a sudden, Marge?" Nick asked.

"You'll find out when we get there," Marjorie told him.

They walked along the stone wall at the edge of the lake. Two boys were fishing. Nick saw a pail beside them on the wall. He went over to it. "Wow! Look at the big sunfish in here, Marge."

"I didn't know there were any that big in the lake," Marjorie said.

The nearest boy stared at Nick. "Are you talking to yourself, kid?"

Nick didn't know what to say. He walked away from the boys. Marjorie ran after him.

The two children went under the

old iron bridge that arched over the lake. They crossed the Long Meadow. Then they followed a little stream until they came to the rear gate of the zoo.

Marjorie always liked to look at the statue of a lioness with cubs. But Nick was walking too fast. He marched over to a big round cage.

"They've got a dog kennel here with raccoons in it," Nick said. "I thought there were birds in this cage."

A zoo keeper was walking by. "There used to be, son. Now the birds are over there." He pointed to a brick building with a row of cages along the outside.

Perched on bare branches in the cages were birds with feathers of every color Nick could imagine.

Marjorie whispered in his ear. "Now you know why we came to the zoo."

19

Marjorie and Nick went over to the red brick building. A downy-headed bird with long tail feathers was walking across the floor of one cage.

"There are five different colors on just that one bird," Nick said. "And all we need are seven feathers!"

"I wonder what kind of bird it is," Marjorie said. "There aren't any signs on the cages."

The zoo man was standing by the door of the building. He couldn't see Marjorie, so he thought it was Nick who had spoken. "That's a golden

pheasant, son. It comes from China."
The man opened the door and went
inside the building.

Nick was looking at the cages.
"There's no way to get into them."

"The keepers have to go in some-
how," Marjorie said. "The gates must
be inside the zoo house."

"The birds keep flying in and out,"
Nick said.

Marjorie laughed. "I guess these
outdoor cages are just like porches for
the ones inside."

A lady standing nearby looked hard
at Nick. Then she picked up her little
boy and hurried away.

"I'm sorry I spoke so loud," Marjorie whispered. "I keep forgetting
people can't see me."

"Let me have the key for a while,"
Nick whispered back. "I'm sick of
everybody thinking I'm crazy."

Marjorie hung the key around Nick's neck. Now he was invisible. He grabbed her hand and pulled her over to the door of the red brick building. Marjorie opened it and went inside.

Nick kept hold of her hand until the door closed behind them.

The air here was hot and damp. No other visitors were in the building.

There was a row of bird cages on one side and a row of monkey cages on the other. The monkeys were all in their outdoor cages today, but some of the birds were indoors.

Marjorie went to look at them. She leaned on a railing to watch three little green parrots and a red-headed macaw. There was a trench between the railing and the cages.

The zoo man was standing in the trench, using a pulley to open a low door in one of the cages. He had to step up from the trench to go through the door. Then he closed the door behind him and went to give the birds fresh water.

Marjorie turned to look at the other cages. They all had doors like this one.

The third cage had a big red parrot with a blue tail in it. The bird was perched on a dead branch. Marjorie remembered the soft green leaves on the trees outdoors. It must be awful to be shut in a cage, she thought.

The parrot flew down to the floor and started to peck at a pan of sunflower seeds. Then, all of a sudden, Marjorie saw the door of the parrot's cage sliding open, as if by itself.

Nick was sneaking into the cage!

20

Majorie saw the door close. Nick must be inside the cage now.

"Squawk!" The beautiful parrot stopped pecking at the sunflower seed. It whirled around, beating its wings and snapping at the air with its big beak.

Something seemed to be holding the bird down, but it yanked itself free and fluttered back to the bare tree branch. The parrot looked all around. Then it set to work to straighten a bent blue feather in its tail.

Marjorie ran over to the railing in front of the parrot's cage. "Nick!" she whispered as loud as she could. "Come out of there!"

The door of the cage slid open. A moment later it closed again.

Marjorie heard a thump as Nick jumped down into the trench in front of the cage. She waited for him to climb out.

The railing shook as Nick hoisted himself over it. "What's the matter, Marge?"

Marjorie was so angry that tears came into her eyes. "Nick, you know better than to do anything like that!"

"I was only going to take one tail feather," Nick said. "That bird would never miss it."

Marjorie felt like shaking her brother, but she didn't know where he was. "It's bad enough for the poor bird to be shut up in a cage without you pulling out its feathers!"

"Well, how did you think we could get the feathers to work the spell?" Nick asked.

Marjorie started to answer, but Nick put his hand over her mouth. "Sh-sh!" he whispered.

The zoo man was walking toward Marjorie. She tried to brush the tears from her eyes.

"Are you all alone, dear?" he asked.

"It's much too hot in here. Only the jungle birds can stand it. The heat makes me dizzy. I thought I heard you talking to somebody." The zoo man rubbed his chin. "I guess I'm tired. It's closing time." He started toward the door. "Come on outside. I have to lock the building."

Marjorie followed the keeper. She walked slowly. Suppose Nick let himself get locked in? Then he could go around yanking feathers without her to stop him. "I'm looking for my little brother," she said. "I know he came into this building. He must be hiding somewhere."

"All right." The keeper went to the door of the building and opened it. "See if you can find him."

"Nick!" Marjorie called.

There was no answer.

Marjorie yelled as loud as she could.

"I'm going home, Nick. And you'd better come with me!"

She heard Nick's voice. It was coming from outdoors. "Marge, come on out here. They're getting ready to shut the gates!"

Marjorie ran to the open door and went out. The zoo man came out after her and locked the door.

"Thank you for letting me call my brother," she said.

The keeper smiled. "It must have been too hot for him in there." He reached into his pocket. "I thought I heard you talking about feathers. I found some beauties in the cages today."

He held out a bunch of the most beautiful feathers Marjorie had ever seen. "Take as many as you like, dear."

21

Marjorie and Nick left the zoo and walked home through the park.

"I'm sorry I fooled with the parrot, Marge," Nick said.

"If you had beautiful tail feathers, you wouldn't want to lose them," Marjorie told him. "You don't even like to have your hair cut."

Nick still had the key. Marjorie was carrying the feathers the zoo man had given her. "I thought there might be some on the ground near the cages," she said. "I never thought of asking for any."

"It sure was nice of the keeper to give them to you," Nick said.

When they came to their front door, Nick unlocked it and gave the key to Marjorie. The children went into the house.

Marjorie ran upstairs to put the key in the glass tray on her dresser. She slipped the feathers into the drawer where she had hidden the witch's spoon. Then she went back downstairs.

Her mother was in the kitchen. "Oh, here you are, Marjorie! I thought I heard both of you children at the door, but I saw only Nick come in. It must be the heat. This has got to be the hottest day of the year."

Marjorie used the kitchen scissors to cut up celery for the tuna-fish salad. Nick set the table in the dining room and turned on the big air conditioner there. Supper was ready by the time Mr. Gordon came home.

Nobody was in a hurry to finish the meal. It was nice and cool in the dining room now. They had ice cream for dessert. Marjorie took tiny bites to make it last as long as possible.

It was dark when supper was over. Mr. Gordon turned on the lights. They all carried their dishes into the kitchen. Mrs. Gordon started the dishwasher. Then everybody went to watch television in the living room.

As soon as Mr. Gordon switched on the set, the lights went out.

"Something's wrong with the fuses," Mr. Gordon said. "I'll have to check the fuse box downstairs." He turned off the air conditioner and the television.

Marjorie pulled the little flashlight out of her jeans pocket. "Use this, Daddy."

Mr. Gordon took the flashlight. He clicked it several times. It didn't go on. "This is worn out, Margie." He gave it back to her.

Mrs. Gordon was busy lighting the candles on the mantle. She picked up one of them. "I'll go down with you, John."

When their parents had gone to the basement, Marjorie and Nick took turns trying the flashlight. Neither of them could get it to work.

"I guess we'll have to magic it again," Nick said. "But how will we light our way down inside the tree?"

"I've got a candle left over from last year's Halloween pumpkin," Marjorie told him.

When Mr. and Mrs. Gordon came back from the basement, Mrs. Gordon said, "We'd better not use any of the air conditioners until the dishwasher has finished. And we'll skip television this evening."

"I have a book I want to read," Marjorie said.

"Don't turn on the ceiling light in your room," her mother warned her. "Use the lamp on your desk. And see if you have a book to keep Nick out of mischief."

Marjorie started up the stairs. Nick came charging behind. "How about that book of riddles?"

Marjorie went to her room. She switched on the little desk light. Nick came in after her. "Marge, is this your house key?" He hung a string with a key on it around his neck.

Marjorie stared at him. "Where did you find it?"

"In this tray on your dresser," Nick said.

Marjorie felt in the tray. It was empty.

She took the key from Nick and hung it around her own neck. "I can see myself in the mirror. The magic must have worn off the key."

"I'm kind of glad," Nick said.

"So am I. It wasn't nearly as much fun as we thought it would be." Marjorie hung the key on her doorknob and went to her bookcase for the book of riddles.

22

"Wake up, Marjorie. It's a beautiful day." Marjorie's mother was shaking her.

Marjorie yawned and stretched. She opened her eyes and looked around the room. Her mother must have gone to wake Nick, she thought. Marjorie couldn't see her anywhere.

The slats on the venetian blind turned to let in the morning sunshine.

Marjorie heard the tap of heels on the floor. She sat up in bed. "Mother!"

"What's the matter?" Mrs. Gordon's voice came from over by the window.

"I lost my house key. Did you find it?" Marjorie jumped out of bed. At once she knew that was the wrong thing to do. Now she might bump into her mother. Marjorie sat down on the bed again.

"I found it, dear." Mrs. Gordon seemed to be coming nearer. "You're lucky. It was quite invisible where you left it on the doorknob. I just happened to touch it. You must be more careful what you do with this key!"

Marjorie felt her mother's hands slip the string over her head. A second later she saw her mother's face. Mrs. Gordon looked as if she were going to faint.

There was no time to lose. Marjorie yanked off the key and dropped it into the bedcovers. She stood up and hugged her mother. "Are you all right?"

Mrs. Gordon blinked. "I am now, but I must have blacked out for a minute."

Marjorie led her mother away from the bed. "Sit in the rocking chair. I'll get you some water."

"Never mind," Mrs. Gordon said. "If you want to do something for me, wake Nick. I have to get your father up. We're late this morning."

Marjorie went down the hall to Nick's room.

He was curled into a ball in the middle of his bed. The air conditioner was on, and Nick had a blanket pulled up to his ears.

"Nick, get up!" Marjorie turned off the air conditioner and pulled down the blanket. "The key is magic again!

It's going to get us into trouble if we don't break the spell."

Nick's eyes were still shut. "Say that again, Marge. What's going on?"

Marjorie told him what had happened. "I promised Mother I'd wake you. Please get up." She ran back to her room to get dressed.

This morning everybody had overslept. Mr. and Mrs. Gordon rushed through breakfast and went off to work before Nick and Marjorie had finished eating.

Marjorie finished her cornflakes and went upstairs to find the key. She thought she'd have a hard time, but as soon as she touched the sheet, she felt the string. A moment later she hung the key around her neck and looked into the mirror.

Marjorie couldn't see herself at all.

23

Marjorie put the key on the glass tray. She took the wooden spoon and the feathers out of the dresser drawer and carried them downstairs.

Nick was still crunching his way through a bowl of Grape-Nuts. "Hey, Marge, I can see you! Couldn't you find the key?"

"I left it upstairs." Marjorie laid the feathers on the table.

Nick counted the colors on his fingers. "Blue, yellow, brown, green, purple, orange, red. That's seven. We ought to be able to work the flying spell."

"I'm not sure I want to," Marjorie told him. "This magic is tricky. Sometimes it works, and sometimes it doesn't."

"Did you try the flashlight today?" Nick asked.

"I left it in the living room." Marjorie went to get the flashlight. She pushed the switch. "Now it's working."

"Maybe we ought to take the Halloween candle along, just in case," Nick said.

Marjorie nodded. "We have to go back to the cave and look in Stella's book. There must be a way to get the spell off the key." She started loading the dishwasher.

Nick ran upstairs. Majorie went down to the laundry room. She found the clothesline and wound it around the wooden spoon.

As she came back up the stairs to the kitchen, Marjorie heard Nick laughing. She couldn't see her brother, but there was an open book on the kitchen table. One of the pages turned over. Nick started to giggle.

"That must be the one about the ostrich," Marjorie said. "Come on, Nick. Let's go to the park. You can read riddles some other time."

The sun flickered through the leaves as the two children climbed the old beech tree. Marjorie went first. When she came to the hole in the tree, she tied one end of the clothesline to a branch and unwound the rest of it from the spoon. "Nick, where are you?"

"Here," Nick said. "Take the key, Marge." He hung it around her neck. At once Marjorie could see him. "Now I can go down the rope without you kicking me in the head," he told her.

Nick grabbed the clothesline and let

himself down into the hole. Marjorie clicked on her flashlight and came after him.

At the bottom of the rope they stepped down into the hollow in the roots of the tree. Marjorie took the key off her neck and tied it to the wooden spoon. As soon as she let go, the key vanished, but Marjorie knew just where it was. She touched it with one finger and the key appeared.

Nick stared at her. "What's going on, Marge? Now I see you. Now I don't."

Marjorie told him what she had done. "This way we can both see each other. That will make it easier to do magic."

She looked for the door in the roots of the tree. It was wide open. "Nick," Marjorie whispered, "I'm *sure* I closed it!"

Nick turned to grab the rope. "Stella must have come back. We'd better get out of here."

At that moment a raspy voice came from the other side of the door. "I was wondering when you two would get here. Come on in."

Marjorie's heart seemed to stop beating. "We'd better do as she says, Nick. She might do something awful to us if we don't."

Marjorie stepped through the doorway. Nick let go of the rope and followed her into the witch's cave.

24

"Look who's here!" Nick said.

The starling was perched on the table beside the book of spells. "Who did you think it was?"

Marjorie was ashamed of how frightened she had been. "Hello," she said to the bird and walked over to put the little square flashlight on the table.

Nick opened the big book and started turning the pages. "Here's the spell for flying, Marge."

Marjorie looked over his shoulder. "You have to hold three feathers in each hand and one in your mouth." She reached into her pocket and pulled out the feathers.

Nick grabbed them.

Marjorie went on reading. "Next you have to step into the brew and go all the way under." She looked across the cave at the steaming pot. "You'd better forget the whole thing, Nick."

"Well, I sure don't want to be boiled," Nick said. He walked over to the pot and touched the brew with the tip of one finger. "Marge, it isn't hot at all!"

"Then why is it steaming?" Marjorie asked.

"Maybe because it's magic." Nick walked back to the table.

Marjorie looked at the book again. "While you're in the brew, you have to tap your head three times with the magic spoon."

Nick laughed. "You'd better do that for me, Marge."

"Don't mess around with that spell," the starling said. "What's so great about flying?"

"You say that because you fly all the time," Nick told the bird. "Come on, Marge." He stuck a feather in his mouth and held three in each hand. Then he ran to the pot and jumped in.

Marjorie rushed over with the wooden spoon. She tapped Nick three times on the head after he went under the brew. "Now, get out of there!"

The brew started to hiss and bubble. The pale gray steam turned blue and then green. For a moment it was bright yellow. A second later it was orange. The orange deepened to red, which became purple and then brown. Finally the pot was covered with steam so black it looked like smoke.

Marjorie couldn't see her brother at all.

After what seemed an age, she heard him splashing. Then a speckled starling climbed onto the rim of the pot and shook the brew from its wings.

It fluttered up into the air. "Hey, Marge, this is great! I'm flying!"

25

The shiny black starling on the table fluffed its feathers. "I warned you!" it said.

Marjorie stopped staring at the bird flying around the room. She went over to the table. For a minute she couldn't speak. Then she said in a very small voice, "You must be Stella."

The starling cocked its head. "Of course!"

"Marge, what happened? You're enormous!" The little speckled starling fluttered down onto the table. It caught sight of the other bird. "Wow! You got bigger too."

"Nobody got *bigger*," the bird told him.

"Nick," Marjorie whispered. "This is *Stella*!"

"Oh." Nick was quiet for a little while. Then he looked down and saw his bird feet. Slowly he turned his head to look first at one wing and then at the other. "I didn't expect to be turned into a bird."

"Neither did I," the witch told him.

"But you're bigger than I am," Nick said. "And you're a much nicer color."

Stella smoothed her shiny feathers with her yellow beak. "You're only a half-grown bird. When you're older, your feathers will turn black with beautiful green and purple lights like mine."

Nick thought about this. He flew up off the table and circled twice around the cave. Then he flew down to perch beside the witch. "It'll be fun to fly home instead of having to walk."

"Mother doesn't like birds in the house," Marjorie reminded him.

"Wait until the sun goes down before you go into your house," Stella said. "The magic doesn't work after dark. You'll be yourself until sunrise."

Marjorie started turning the pages of the big book. "Where's the page that tells you how to break the spells?"

"There isn't a page like that in the book," the witch said.

"You mean we have to stay like this?" Nick asked.

"Only in the daytime," Stella told him. "Never mind. You'll get used to it. I had to figure out how to get back in here. I can't open the door when I'm a bird, but I can fly down inside the tree and wait till night comes." She looked pleased with herself.

"Mom will be mad at me if I'm late for dinner every night," Nick said. "And she won't like finding a bird in my bed in the morning."

Marjorie was still reading the book. "There's a spell here that would turn you into a cat. Mother likes cats."

"Do you think your mother would let you keep two cats?" the witch asked. "I'd rather eat meat loaf than mulberries."

Nick turned to look at her. "Did you work the flying spell all by yourself, Stella?"

The starling nodded. "The only hard part was banging myself on the head. I had to let the spoon float in the brew and come up from under it."

"That was quite a trick," Nick said.

"I'm sorry now that I bothered," the witch told him.

Marjorie was staring at the wooden spoon. It was still damp from the magic brew. She held it up. "Nick, look!"

"I can see the key!" Nick said.

Marjorie untied the key and hung it around her neck.

"I can see you too, Marge. What does it mean?" Nick asked.

"Do you remember what happened to the shoelace when it went into the brew a second time?" Marjorie said.

"You mean that's all it takes to break a spell?" Nick asked. Then he yelled, "Come on, Stella! Last one in the brew is a rotten egg!"

26

Nick and Stella winged their way across the cave and splashed into the steaming pot. The magic brew foamed over their heads. Marjorie ran over to stir it with the wooden spoon.

"Ready or not, here I come!" Nick climbed out of the pot. "How do I look, Marge?"

"Wet," Marjorie told him.

Nick looked down at his blue jeans and sneakers. He stretched out his arms and wiggled his fingers. "I'm going to miss those wings."

Majorie turned to look at the pot. A black point was rising out of it. This was the top of Stella's hat. A second later Marjorie saw the wide brim. Bubbly drops of brew dripped

from it over the witch's face. She had
bright green eyes, a long thin nose,
and a pointed chin. Her straggly hair
was as black as her hat.

Marjorie had forgotten how scary
Stella had looked at the window. She
watched the witch's bony fingers grab
the rim of the pot as she climbed
out. Stella seemed to get bigger and

bigger. Marjorie wanted to run, but she couldn't move.

Stella's buckled shoes thumped down on the dirt floor of the cave. She shook out the wet folds of her long black dress. Then she stretched out her skinny hand. "If you don't mind, Marjorie, I'd like my spoon back."

Marjorie was sure that the witch would be much more dangerous when she had her magic spoon. And maybe she was angry because Nick and Marjorie had been using it. But the spoon did belong to Stella. Marjorie handed it to her. "Are you still going to use it after what happened?"

Stella's thin face cracked into a smile. Her green eyes sparkled. "I've had lots of fun with magic," she said. "I don't know what I'd do without it. Besides, now I know how to break the spells." She rubbed her pointed chin. "At least I think I do. With magic you never can be sure of anything."

The witch walked over to the pile of dry leaves. She pulled a black broom from under the tattered blanket. "The trouble with this," she said, "is that it only flies at night."

"Why?" Nick asked.

"Because I worked the spell at night," Stella told him.

"Nick and I have to go home for lunch," Marjorie said. "Do you want to join us, Stella?"

"I'd like to," the witch said, "but people always seem to stare at me. I'd rather be out when most of them are asleep. It was nice of you to ask me, Marjorie. I hope you and Nick will visit me sometimes."

"That would be fun," Nick said.

Stella yawned. "Don't come too early

in the day. I usually go to bed at sunrise."

"We'll wait until afternoon." Marjorie picked up the flashlight and walked to the door.

Nick followed her out to the hollow in the roots of the tree. His clothes were still soaking wet. "I'm glad I had a chance to fly, Marge, even if it didn't last long." He grabbed hold of the clothesline and started to shinny up.

Marjorie climbed up the rope after him. She shined the flashlight up into the hollow trunk of the tree.

"Marge!" Nick yelled. "You'd better hang on tight. Somebody's pulling up the rope!"

27

The clothesline rose up through the hollow tree, dragging Nick and Marjorie with it.

When they came out of the hole in the trunk, Marjorie looked around to see who had pulled them up. But there was no one there. She clicked off her flashlight and put it into her pocket. Then she untied the rope from the tree branch.

"Too bad you had to give the spoon back, Marge," Nick said. "Now we don't have anything to wind the rope on. How are we going to keep it from getting tangled?"

The clothesline stretched out and floated in the air.

Marjorie stared at it. "Some of the

magic in the spoon must have rubbed off on it," she whispered.

Nick touched the rope with one finger. "It's damp from the magic brew in my clothes. Do you suppose that could have done the trick?"

"Maybe." Marjorie gently stroked the clothesline. "Stella said with magic you never can be sure of anything."

"At least we know it's magic," Nick said. "I wonder what it can do."

"Ropey," Marjorie asked, "could you take us home?"

The clothesline gave a happy little wiggle and rubbed against Marjorie's arm.

Marjorie and Nick held onto the rope with their hands and twisted their legs around it. The clothesline sailed up out of the old beech tree. It flew high over Prospect Park and across the roofs of Brooklyn.

In almost no time Nick and Marjorie landed on their own front stoop.

Marjorie gave the clothesline a little pat. "Thank you, Ropey." She looped it over her arm.

"We'll have to be careful, Marge," Nick said. "The clothesline probably can't fly after the sun goes down."

"Mother doesn't like us to be out after dark anyway." Marjorie opened the door with her house key. "Now let's see what we can have for lunch."

Other books by Ruth Chew

Earthstar Magic (Hardcover: Hastings House)
The Hidden Cave
 (Hardcover: Hastings House, as *The Magic Cave*)
The Magic Coin
Magic in the Park
Mostly Magic
No Such Thing as a Witch
 (Hardcover: Hastings House)
Second-Hand Magic (Hardcover: Holiday House)
The Secret Summer
 (original title: *Baked Beans for Breakfast*)
Summer Magic
The Trouble with Magic (Hardcover: Dodd Mead)
The Wednesday Witch (Hardcover: Holiday House)
What the Witch Left (Hardcover: Hastings House)
The Wishing Tree (Hardcover: Hastings House)
Witch in the House (Hardcover: Hastings House)
Witch's Broom (Hardcover: Dodd Mead)
The Witch's Buttons (Hardcover: Hastings House)
The Witch's Garden (Hardcover: Hastings House)
The Would-Be Witch (Hardcover: Hastings House)